Dear Parents:

Congratulations! Your child is taking the first steps on an exciting journey. The destination? Independent reading!

STEP INTO READING® will help your child get there. The program offers five steps to reading success. Each step includes fun stories and colorful art or photographs. In addition to original fiction and books with favorite characters, there are Step into Reading Non-Fiction Readers, Phonics Readers and Boxed Sets, Sticker Readers, and Comic Readers—a complete literacy program with something to interest every child.

Learning to Read, Step by Step!

Ready to Read   Preschool–Kindergarten
• big type and easy words • rhyme and rhythm • picture clues
For children who know the alphabet and are eager to begin reading.

Reading with Help   Preschool–Grade 1
• basic vocabulary • short sentences • simple stories
For children who recognize familiar words and sound out new words with help.

Reading on Your Own   Grades 1–3
• engaging characters • easy-to-follow plots • popular topics
For children who are ready to read on their own.

Reading Paragraphs   Grades 2–3
• challenging vocabulary • short paragraphs • exciting stories
For newly independent readers who read simple sentences with confidence.

Ready for Chapters   Grades 2–4
• chapters • longer paragraphs • full-color art
For children who want to take the plunge into chapter books but still like colorful pictures.

STEP INTO READING® is designed to give every child a successful reading experience. The grade levels are only guides; children will progress through the steps at their own speed, developing confidence in their reading.

Remember, a lifetime love of reading starts with a single step!

BARBIE and associated trademarks and trade dress are owned by, and used under license from, Mattel.
©2021 Mattel.
www.barbie.com

Published in the United States by Random House Children's Books, a division of Penguin Random House LLC, 1745 Broadway, New York, NY 10019, and in Canada by Penguin Random House Canada Limited, Toronto.

Step into Reading, Random House, and the Random House colophon are registered trademarks of Penguin Random House LLC.

Visit us on the Web!
StepIntoReading.com
rhcbooks.com

Educators and librarians, for a variety of teaching tools, visit us at RHTeachersLibrarians.com

ISBN 978-0-593-37359-0 (trade) — ISBN 978-0-593-37360-6 (lib. bdg.)
Printed in the United States of America

10 9 8 7 6 5 4 3 2 1

Barbie™

YOU CAN BE A MUSICIAN

by Christy Webster
illustrated by Fernando Güell,
Ferran Rodriguez, and David Güell

Random House 🏠 New York

Barbie loves music.

So does her friend Daisy.

They go to a concert.
Their favorite pop star
is Melody.

"I wish we could write a song," Barbie says. "Melody can help," says Ameera. She is Melody's manager.

Barbie and Daisy
meet Melody!

Melody tells Barbie
to start with lyrics.
Lyrics are the words
in a song.

Barbie writes down
the words
she wants to sing.

Melody helps Barbie

add music to her words.

She plays piano.

Barbie plays guitar.

They try many ideas.
They work until
they like their new song.

Bradley hears
the new song.

She is a music producer.

She records

Barbie's song.

Bradley shows Barbie
how she records.

First, she records each part.

Then she uses her computer
to mix them together.

Daisy tries the turntable.

She creates a beat

for Barbie's song.

It is time to record!
First, they record
the guitar and
piano music.

Then Barbie enters
the vocal booth.
They will record
her singing.
It is so quiet inside!

Melody helps Barbie
warm up her voice.
They sing high
and low notes.

Barbie puts on headphones.

She hears Daisy's beat.

She hears the guitar
and piano.

She sings the song.

Everyone loves

Barbie's singing!

Bradley shows Daisy
how she mixes the song.
She puts the parts together.
She makes changes.
It sounds great!

Melody has an idea.
Barbie and Daisy
will perform their new
song at her next concert!

Barbie and Daisy
practice all week.

Before the concert,
Barbie and Daisy
rehearse with the band.

The band quickly learns
Barbie's new song.

They play
the song together.
They practice
the song many times.

They want
to be ready
for the concert.

Before the concert,

Daisy is nervous.

"You can do it,"

Barbie says.

Barbie and Daisy
practice one more time.
They are ready!

Everyone loves
Barbie and Daisy's song.
"You are musicians!"
Melody says.